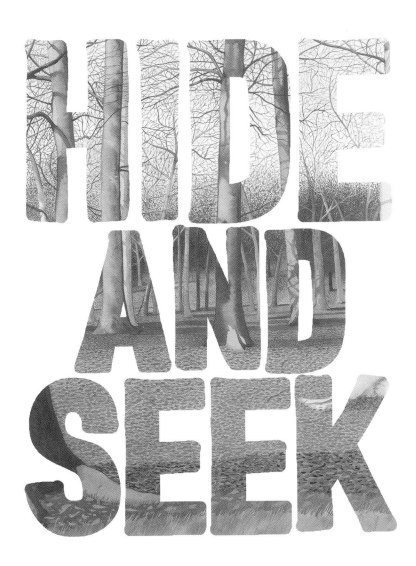

For Hanne

First U.S. edition 2018

Library of Congress Catalog Card Number pending
ISBN 978-1-5362-0260-1

18 19 20 21 22 23 TLF 10 9 8 7 6 5 4 3 2 1

Printed in Dongguan, Guangdong, China

This book was typeset in Poliphilus.

Candlewick Press
99 Dover Street
Somerville, Massachusetts 02144

visit us at www.candlewick.com

HIDE AND SEEK

Anthony Browne

CANDLEWICK PRESS

Poppy and Cy had been sad ever since
their dog, Goldie, had disappeared.
They sat . . .

and sat . . .
and thought about what to do.
"We should play something," said Cy.

"What about cards?" asked Poppy.

"Boring!" said Cy. "I want to play monsters!"

"Monsters are **stupid**," said Poppy. "Why don't we go outside?"

"But what **will** we play?" asked Cy.

"**You** come up with something," said Poppy.

"How about hide–and–seek?" said Cy.

"OK," said Poppy. "Why don't you go into the woods,
and then I'll come and look for you."

Cy ran off as Poppy counted.

"One, two, three, four . . ."

"five, six,

eight . . .,"

seven,

Cy ran deep into the forest
and found a tangle of branches.

This is a good place, he thought.
She'll **never** *find me here.*

"Nine . . . ten . . . Ready or not, here I come!"

Poppy finished counting and strolled into the woods.

Cy was excited — he was so well hidden!
He knew he had to be quiet,

but he couldn't stop shaking.

Poppy thought she'd find Cy quickly —
he always chose easy places to hide.
He's probably behind that tree . . .

But he wasn't.

Oh, no, thought Cy. *I think I need to pee!*
Why does this always happen when I hide?
I wonder if Poppy will find me soon. . . .

But Poppy was still a long way away.

He can't have gone far, she thought.
Maybe he's hiding behind that pile of logs.

But he wasn't.

Will it be too hard for Poppy to find me here? thought Cy.

Where was Cy? *Maybe he's behind that fallen tree. . . .*

He wasn't.

I wish she'd come and find me, thought Cy.
I hope she hasn't gone home and left me.

*He **must** be over there,* thought Poppy.

He wasn't.

I'm getting cold now, thought Cy.
I want to go home.

*I didn't want him to come this **far** into the woods,* thought Poppy.

What's that noise?

What's that noise?

"Found you! Both of you!
I was getting worried," said Poppy.

"I was worried, too," said Cy,
"but Goldie's back and now everything is OK!"

"Let's go home," said Poppy.

So they all did, together.

What else is hiding in the forest?
Did you see . . .

an armchair?

a bone?

some cans?

a dog collar?

a crocodile?

some dogs?

a duck?

an ear?

an elephant's trunk?

some faces?

a giraffe?

a hat?

a leash?

a paw?

a spear?

a faucet?

a trumpet?

a cane?

There's lots more to find!